'TWAS TWO WEEKS TIL...

'Twas Two Weeks Til...

A Holiday Romance

SHARHONDA L. SHARP

SLS Publishing, LLC

Contents

Copyright	vi
Dedication	vii
1. 'Twas two weeks til'...	1
2. 'Twas still two weeks til...	9
3. 'Twas ten days til...	14
4. 'Twas six days til...	28
5. 'Twas the night of...	44
6. 'Twas a fairy tale ending...	62
About The Author	68

Copyright © 2024 by ShaRhonda Lynnette Sharp

All rights reserved. No part of this book may be reproduced in any manner or any electronic or mechanical means, including information storage and retrieval systems whatsoever without written permission except in the case of brief quotations embodied in critical articles and reviews.

This book is a work of fiction. Names, characters, business, organizations, places, events and incidents are the product of the author's imagination or are used fictitiously. Any similarities to persons, living or dead; events or locations is entirely coincidental.

Contact Info: slsthepassionatescribe@gmail.com

Cover Design: SLS Publishing, LLC
Editor: SLS Publishing, LLC
First Printing, 2024

'Tis always the Season,
No matter the Reason,
To always have the Audacity
To believe in Love.

Chapter 1

'Twas two weeks til'...

The chimes of the elevator ascending one floor after another inside Willis Tower blended with the early morning chatter of fellow office arrivers and surrounded Leticia Nadal as she crammed in for her thirty-four floor ride. She was mentally rattling off her checklist for what needed to be done today as she periodically shifted her stance to allow passengers on and off at their respective floors. It was Monday, which officially put her at the two week mark before the Mayor's Christmas Masquerade Party in this very building.

The Mayor's Director of Community Affairs, who also happened to be her brother-in-law, Hector, personally commissioned Leticia to coordinate an extravagant, yet charitable, affair. She excitedly accepted the project back in October, but now with her deadline creeping closer and closer, that "Grinch" known as stress and anxiety she had been able to ignore before was finally digging its nails in.

The flashing green numbers entranced Leticia as she continued mumbling her to-do list to herself. The doors parted at her floor and she was met with the immediate bombardment of morning greetings and holiday radio blaring from the overhead speakers. Leticia smiled and waved politely, like she did every morning, as she continued the trek to her courtesy office.

The Director of Building Operations had provided Leticia a stationary workspace for the last six weeks leading up to the event to help make her life easier in overseeing the site and her team, of which she was extremely grateful. She noticed the door was already propped open, indicating her assistant, De'Vyne, had beat her into the office.

"Good morning, Gorgeous!" Leticia sang as she entered the office.
"Good morning, Boss Lady! Happy Monday!" De'Vyne greeted in Spanish with a huge grin across his face.
"Oh! Well, happy Monday to you, too! How was your weekend?" she responded back in Spanish with a proud smile.
"It was great, despite the snow. Not that it stopped me," he continued with a wink.
"Ooh! Look at you! I see them *Babbel* courses have been paying off, huh?"
"You see me?!"

Leticia bursts into joyous giggles as she high-fived her assistant. When De'Vyne first started working for her, he said since she was half Black and half Dominican he wanted to learn Spanish to speak to Leticia in her other native language sometimes.

"Gotta give you a taste of home after code-switching all day, ya know?" he would often say.

De'Vyne was a beautiful, brown skinned, bearded, meticulously well-kempt, mildly flamboyant Black man with the most exquisite makeup skills Leticia had ever seen. He had joined her team about six months ago, and she was so glad, too; because when the Mayor's office came calling, he was the loudest voice cheering her on and jumping in to help at every moment, even without her having to ask. There was nothing he wouldn't do to ensure she succeeded at the biggest event of her career.

"Here is your calendar, presentation deck and favorite purple clipboard with today's checklist," De'Vyne presented the items stacked neatly on the corner of his desk.
"Ugh! Bless you!" Leticia sighed heavily as she slipped out of her coat and hung it up.
"Okay, outfit!" he praised, snapping his fingers.

Leticia wore a long red and black checkered tweed blazer over a cream colored flowy jumpsuit and red pumps. A lengthy silver necklace with multicolored stones hung down to her diaphragm and matching earrings dangled along the sides of her face. Her long, dark curly hair was pulled back into a wavy ponytail, and she donned her favorite burgundy lipstick that unlocked her "Baddie" attitude every time. Leticia spun around, showing off every angle and posing like a runway model as she laughed giddily.

She blew De'Vyne a kiss when he handed over her Christmas-themed thermos filled with piping hot peppermint mocha fresh from the *Keurig* behind him. She asked if he'd been upstairs to walk the event site yet, because she was anxious to know what progress had been made by the decorators. He said he hadn't, but would run up while she was in her meeting with Hector and his team giving them status updates on everything.

"And *yes*, I will take pictures and send them to you," Dc'Vync confirmed with a wide grin, batting his medium mink eyelashes
"And video!" Leticia quipped, pointing a rose gold stiletto fingernail his way.
"Yes, ma'am!" he replied with a laugh.
"Have you seen Emilio today?" she asked about the sound and lighting engineer they were working with.
"I haven't, actually."
"He hasn't answered any of my calls or texts the last couple days either."

De'Vyne assured her he'd track down Emilio when he went upstairs and bring her a full report of everything as he headed out. Leticia gathered her meeting materials, cellphone and coffee and prepared to leave, as well. Before walking out, she stopped at the full length mirror behind the door. After assessing her reflection and being satisfied with what she saw, Leticia looked herself in the eyes and gave a quick pep talk.

"*You* are fucking dope! *You* are the bomb! *You* deserve to be here! *You* are the best person for the job and every-fucking-body knows it! If they don't, they will! You're Leticia Nadal, dammit!"

Leticia gave a confident nod and smile to her reflection then marched out of her office and down the hall to the conference room, strutting just as boldly as she felt.

"What the hell is this?!" Leticia barked in a high voice as she entered the open event space.

De'Vyne had sent photos as promised, and what she saw made it nearly impossible to keep her composure during her meeting. The team of contracted decorators were in the process of hanging giant ornaments from the ceiling and wrapping the banisters and balconies in tinsel and strings of lights when Leticia walked in. The problem was the entire color scheme they had going was all off and nothing close to what she originally instructed them to do.

"Boss Lady, it's okay. I got it," De'Vyne tried to reassure her.
"Dev, what the hell?! *How* the hell?!" Leticia exclaimed each question as she swept her arms through the air in confusion.
"I have no idea, but I'll take care of it," he promised.
"We are down to the wire here. We ain't got time for this mess!"
"I know. I know. I'll handle it. You got enough to deal with. Let me get this."

Leticia begrudgingly conceded and demanded this issue be resolved by Wednesday at the latest because they had a very tight schedule to keep. De'Vyne nodded his understanding and made his way over to the huddle of contractors, gruffly barking orders as he went. She called after him, asking if he'd run into Emilio yet, and he said he still hadn't seen him.

"Where the hell is he?" Leticia mumbled to herself as she pulled her cellphone out to call him again.

This time it went straight to voicemail and a small twinge of panic set in until she turned the corner and saw a man inside the electrical closet with his back to the door. She released a sigh of relief and quickly began rattling off her list of expectations.

"Good morning, Emilio," Leticia said, trying to mask her annoyance and looking down at her clipboard. "Hope you're ready to work today, because we have a lot to do. First thing's first, we need to do a walkthrough to make sure all the sockets are operable and make a final decision on where the cords will run."

Leticia continued robotically naming things on her checklist and asking for updates on certain items, but stopped when she realized Emilio still hadn't said a word.

"Emilio, you haven't answered any of my questions," Leticia commented, now dropping her pseudo-pleasant tone.
"Probably because *Emilio* ain't here," the man said sarcastically, finally turning to face her.
"*Domino*," she exhaled in a breathy whisper of surprise.

The coverall-clad man with his hat turned backwards narrowed his gaze in suspicion as he looked at Leticia. He tilted his head to the left and twisted his mouth as if in deep contemplation. Who was this woman calling him by such a familiar name only reserved for those closest to him?

"I know you?" he asked in a gravelly voice.
"Yeah...I mean, you used to," Leticia replied nervously. "We went to Jefferson High together. It's Leticia."
"*Tecie*?!" he asked in a shocked tone, his eyes wide.

"Oh, wow. Haven't heard that name in years."
"Yeah, neither have I."

Dominic "Domino" Ballantyne lowered his lids, taking his gaze from shocked to intrigued. He drank in the sight of the woman standing in front him, letting his eyes roam over her face as if re-committing it to memory. She mostly looked the same, but there was a certain mature edginess about her now that he was immediately drawn to like a moth to a flame.

He emerged from the electrical closet, making Leticia take several steps backward, as she tried to regulate her nervous breathing. Of all the people in Chicago — in the *world* — Dominic "Domino" Ballantyne was the absolute last person she'd ever expected to run into. It had been over ten years since she'd last seen him, and she still practically drooled at the sight of him.

Dominic had the most gorgeous golden brown complexion that was practically flawless, except for a light patch of skin forming a birthmark around his left eye. A shadowy beard covered his strong jaw and encircled blush pink lips; and full thick eyebrows hovered above deep brown eyes.

Even though his jumpsuit looked oversized, Leticia could vividly see the broad expanse of his chest and shoulders, and quietly wondered what other secrets his uniform was hiding?

The feel of Dominic's hand cupping her elbow made Leticia snap out of her trance. She blinked slowly as the entirety of his face came back into view and she remembered where she was and what she was doing.

"You good?" Dominic asked softly.

"Huh? Yeah, I'm good," Leticia replied, her words coming out faster than normal. "Uh, wh-what are you doing here?"

"That's what I'm trying to figure out, actually," he said, his mouth twisting up again.

"Where is Emilio? He hasn't responded to any of my calls or texts and I need him here ASAP."

"Yeah, he ain't responding to anybody. As luck would have it, Emilio got himself a winning lottery ticket last week and disappeared without a word."

"What?!"

Chapter 2

'Twas still two weeks til...

Dominic informed Leticia that Emilio had skipped town without word or warning, leaving him to inherit a bulk of the workload left behind. The problem was that all of Emilio's projects were "in progress," and there was no way of finding out what had already been done, what else needed to be done or what the final results were supposed to be without asking the client. Something Dominic hated doing because he always felt it made him look incompetent. This time was no different.

"I'm trying to figure out what the hell was *he doing* so I know what *I need* to do, but it's looking easier said than done," Dominic said as he huffed in frustration and shoved his hands in the pockets of his jumpsuit.

"This can't be happening!" Leticia exclaimed, no longer able to withhold her panic.

"It's not as bad as it looks, " he replied, trying hard to sound convincing.

"No, you don't understand," she said frantically. "This is the biggest event of my career. I can't *not* pull this off, and the last thing I need is people going M.I.A. *Especially* now!"

Leticia slammed her clipboard and cellphone down on a nearby table and began pacing back and further, murmuring and cursing in Spanish as she went. *First the décor fiasco and now this! What the hell else could possibly go wrong?!* she thought to herself. Her heels collided angrily with the floor tiles as she exhaled one heavy breath after another between grumbles and murmurs.

Leticia stopped pacing long enough to reign herself in by remembering the mantra she said in the mirror mere hours ago. Taking a deep breath and releasing it slowly, she turned on her heels to face Dominic, who was now standing directly behind her. He caught her by the waist, barely stopping them from crashing into each other, and her hands landed on his chest. Their eyes met and for a moment everything around them faded to black.

His strong hands gripped her sides, sinking his fingertips into the softness of her flesh beneath the thin fabric of her jumpsuit. Leticia's fingers flexed against the material of Dominic's coveralls, feeling the firmness of his chest and steadiness of his heartbeat underneath. His eyes dropped to her mouth when he saw the tip of her tongue dart out and swipe across her parted lips, making him swallow hard.

"It's okay," Dominic said softly, blinking slowly and bringing his eyes back to hers. "Short notice and tight deadlines are my specialty. I got you. I promise."

"Okay," Leticia whispered as a slight smile formed on her lips.

Dominic gave a comforting wink before taking a step back, letting his fingers drag along Leticia's curves as he released the hold he had on her. Her breath shuddered in her throat at the sensation of his hands grazing her body, and she instantly felt an emptiness when he was no longer touching her.

"So," Dominic started as he put his now empty hands back into his pockets. "I just need a little time to figure out where Emilio left off, and I can take it from there."

"Oh, um...I can help with that," Leticia chimed in after regaining her composure. "If you remember, I was the one who always took notes and wrote down everything."

Leticia went over to the table where she'd slammed down her things and rifled through the pile, retrieving a legal pad and the presentation deck from her meeting earlier. She flipped through the legal pad until she found her notes from all the previous walkthroughs with Emilio and ripped out the pages.

"These are very detailed, but easy to follow, I promise," Leticia explained with a soft chuckle. "And there are photos of everything in this PowerPoint to give you a visual. I hope this helps."

"Tecie Nadal saving my life, once again," Dominic said with a smirk as he flipped through the pages.

"If you're as good as you say, then you'll be saving my life, too."

"I am."

Leticia turned her head to hide the smile and redness flushing across her face. She gathered her things and told Dominic she'd leave him alone to get to work.

"My, uh, number is, uh, on the first page of that presentation," Leticia informed him as she started backing away to leave. "If you need anything, just call or text me. I'm pretty much attached to this phone now."

"I'll definitely call you," Dominic said, his deep, raspy voice smothering each word in a sensuality he didn't even bother to hide.

Leticia was so stunned by his definite tone and the flirty glint in his eyes that she lost all ability to speak, and just settled for an awkward wave as she rushed to walk away. She was walking so fast, she almost crashed into De'Vyne, who was watching her like a hawk.

"Oh, hey. Did you get the decorators sorted out?" Leticia asked, trying to sound professional.

"Yeah, I did," De'Vyne said dryly with his eyes narrowed and hands on his hips. "Now *who* and *what* the hell was that?"

"Excuse me?" she asked, her eyes quickly darting back and forth.

"I saw you letting that man feel you up back there! Now who is *him*?"

"Huh? Oh, that's Domi..*nic*...and he was not feeling me up!"

Leticia swatted at De'Vyne playfully as she brushed past him and started towards the elevator. He kept pace with her, probing her with one question after another about the handsome stranger he spotted with her, and she ignored every one of them. All she would say is he was the new sound and lighting engineer replacing Emilio since he had vanished without a trace.

"Sound and lighting, huh? Well, I definitely saw a spark," De'Vyne said coyly with a sneaky smile, cutting his eyes at her.

"Oh, hush!" Leticia chastised jokingly as she watched the numbers of the elevator for what already felt like the hundredth time today.

Leticia clutched the clipboard tightly to her chest as she quietly reflected on the feel of Dominic's warm hands on her body. Even though the moment was brief, it felt like time stood still and nothing else mattered except their closeness. There was a time when she used to dream of such a moment to be shared with Thee Domino Ballantyne, but now that she had, she wanted more. Leticia let out a dejected sigh as she stepped off the elevator because she knew that the desires and musings of her inner lovesick teenaged self were just that – fleeting and never gonna happen.

Chapter 3

'Twas ten days til...

"Isn't that what you pay other people to do?" a distinct voice called out from below.

Leticia groaned and rolled her eyes before plastering a fake smile on her face as she looked down at her big sister, Edie, who was looking up with an unmistakable scowl of disgust.

"Hello to you too, Edie," Leticia said sarcastically. "And sometimes when you want it done right you have to do it yourself."

Leticia was on a ladder hanging strings of garland from the base of the balcony, draping them in loops as she went, when her sister arrived. They were supposed to be going to lunch, but she knew the real reason Edie came by was to spy on the progress being made with the Christmas party. Especially, since her husband's good name and reputation were attached to it.

Edie was apprehensive about the decision to use Leticia in the first place, but she was outvoted. Her husband, Hector, fully believed in his sister-in-law's skills for curating epic events, just based on her previous work. So, when he was tasked with putting something together for the Mayor's office, Leticia was the first call he made, much to Edie's chagrin. Even though she told him it was a good idea, she wasn't really on board, and her not-so-random pop-up visits were proof of that.

Leticia could see through Edie's false niceties of lunch invites and supply drop offs like glass, but opted not to let on that she knew her sister's true motives. She'd much rather successfully pull off this Christmas party without a hitch and gloat about proving Edie wrong later than argue with her now.

"You're early," Leticia said, looking at her watch after descending the ladder.
"Well, I was already in the area," Edie replied with a shrug.
"Already in the area? You live in Wicker Park," Leticia replied skeptically with a side-eye.
"What did I say?" Edie snapped, putting her hands on her hips.

Leticia rolled her eyes and said she couldn't leave right now because she was in the middle of a project. Edie huffed about them having this lunch date scheduled well-enough in advance that she shouldn't be getting excuses right now.

"It's not an excuse. You came too early," Leticia said flatly with a shrug as she climbed the ladder again.
"Oh, really, Late-ticia? Being too early is a problem, now?" Edie tossed back, rolling her neck and narrowing her eyes.
"You know I hate when you call me that!" Leticia exclaimed, nearly dropping the nail gun she was holding. "I was late *one* time! Let it go!"
"Nope."

As the two sisters continued their spat, the sound of Leticia's raised voice traveled across the room and caught Dominic's attention, making him pop up from inside the raised platform that would be the DJ's booth. He looked over to where the women were and his eyes immediately became fixed on the curvature of Leticia's hips and butt in her dark blue jeans and the sliver of skin of her lower back that peeked out beneath the hem of her sweater each time she raised her arms.

Dominic licked and bit his bottom lip as he studied her every move. He didn't care at all if anyone else saw him watching her. Nothing could tear his eyes away from the woman who had swirled back into his life like a bodacious blizzard, taking his breath away at every turn. He looked forward to hearing her voice every day, even if it was just her rambling about her many checklists and deadlines. And her laugh? Music to his ears. However, right now there was a harshness in her tone that Dominic didn't like, because that meant someone was messing with "his Tecie Baby."

His brows knitted together as he frowned in anger, trying to figure out who the mystery woman was getting under Leticia's skin. Just then, Edie turned around and locked eyes with Dominic and he groaned loudly before crouching back down behind the DJ booth to finish working on the cords and switchboard.

"Is that..." Edie's voice trailed off as she squinted her eyes to make out the face she'd just seen across the room. "Leticia, tell me you did not hire that degenerate?"

"Who are you talking about?" Leticia grunted over her shoulder as she placed the last nail in the base to hang the rest of the garland.

"*Domino Ballantyne,*" his name rolled off her tongue with such disdain.

"Oh...uh...yeah, he's the engineer," Leticia stated shyly.
"*Engineer*?! *Him*?! Not likely."
"Wow, Edie!"

The sound of approaching footsteps made them both turn around and Leticia instantly began smiling at how Dominic made something as simple as walking look so damn sexy. He had gotten a fresh haircut recently so his handsome face was no longer covered by a baseball cap. Just the dewy glistening that sweat leaves behind after a long hard day of work — a look Leticia was becoming more and more grateful for.

"Hey, Tecie," Dominic interrupted the sisters' quarrel. "Here are your notes back from a few days ago. I keep forgetting to give them to you."
"Who the hell is *Tecie*?" Edie asked with a frown.

Dominic cut his eyes at her, never uttering a word as he passed her and stood at the base of the ladder. His scowl was steady as he slowly pulled his eyes away from Edie's face to look up at Leticia, who he quickly and sweetly smiled at as he handed over the papers. She smiled back as she came down the ladder, stopping on the rung that brought her eye level to him.

Edie watched the silent exchange between the two of them and scoffed loudly, making Dominic's head snap back around to glare in her direction again. Leticia nervously dropped her eyes to the floor, wishing she could just liquify and disappear between the cracks.

"Always good to see you, Edith," Dominic snarled, using her real name.
"It's *Edie*, to you," she snarled in return.

"And it's *Dominic*, to you," he said sternly, looking her up and down and letting her know he'd heard her earlier comments about him.

Edie snorted and rolled her eyes as she waved him off and turned away from them. Leticia mouthed an apology to Dominic, who shook his head to say that wasn't necessary. He told her he needed to run out to his truck to get some more wiring for the DJ booth and grab a bite to eat. When Dominic asked if she wanted anything, Edie cut him off to say she was taking Leticia to lunch and that he needed to be more concerned with doing his actual job.

"Edie!" Leticia exclaimed, going red from embarrassment.
"Leticia, don't be letting this...whatever you're supposed to be...get away with murder just 'cuz you're still carrying a torch for him," Edie said dismissively. "He is an *employee*. Treat him like one."
"Oh, my God! Domino, I am so sorry for this," Leticia apologized profusely, grabbing his arm. "You can go. Take all the time you need. It's okay."

Dominic looked up at the ceiling, drew in a deep inhale and nodded his head as he exhaled a long, heavy breath — trying his hardest to keep his rage in check and not lash out at the woman hellbent on rubbing him the wrong way. He looked over at Leticia who was still clinging to his arm, and suddenly the comfort of that feeling settled the angry fire blazing inside him.

Dominic didn't want to leave Leticia's embrace, but knew he needed to get away from her sister as soon as possible. He nodded again and slipped out of Leticia's hands, brushing past Edie and glaring at her once more before leaving.

"What is wrong with you?!" Leticia asked angrily in Spanish as she slammed the stack of papers onto the utility cart beside her.

"Me?! What's wrong with you?!" Edie hurled back at her in Spanish. "Why would you let someone like *that* work with you? See, I knew it was a bad idea to have you do this party. Do you know who your client is?"

"Tell me how you really feel, Edie," Leticia said flippantly.

"Okay, I think you're in over your head with all of this, and you're trying so hard to prove a point, that you're making piss poor business decisions, like working with the boy who terrorized our neighborhood for years."

"He terrorized *you*. He was always nice to me. And anyway, his past is none of my business. He's working now and he's actually very good at his job. Just like *I'm* damn good at *my* job. Not that you'd ever bother to notice."

Leticia grabbed a box of figurines and statuettes off the floor and marched to the other side of the room to begin placing the centerpieces on the tall tables situated around the perimeter. It was now ten days until the big day. Her catering team was coming tomorrow to finalize the menu, do a walk-through to get a feel for the space, and plan out how they'd navigate once it was filled with some of Illinois' political and social elite.

This week alone, she had a full schedule with one vendor partner after another coming to the site to discuss all the particulars, which was stressful enough. The last thing she needed was Edie and any of her bullshit.

"You can go," Leticia said with her back still turned. "I've got a lot to do and don't have time for lunch right now."

"Lettie, you have to eat at some point. This stuff can wait," Edie said, rolling her eyes.

"Bye, Edie," Leticia snapped as she moved to the next table to set up more centerpieces.

Edie looked at the back of her sister's head in disbelief. She waited silently for Leticia to say something...anything...but she stayed quiet and kept on working. So, Edie loudly smacked her lips, gave a dry "Adios," and left without another word – much to Leticia's relief.

A light knock on her office door broke through Leticia's concentration while she was updating the PowerPoint with new photos of today's progress. Her heart skipped a beat when she saw Dominic standing there, bathed in the late afternoon sunlight streaming through the hall window behind him.

He had changed out of his coveralls into a beige fitted, long-sleeved thermal shirt; dark blue slim-fit jeans and wheat Timberland boots. His close cropped dark hair glistened, but they didn't hold a candle to the glint in his beautiful brown eyes that seemed to pierce her soul every time he looked at her.

"Hi," Leticia exhaled just above a whisper.

"Hi," Dominic's voice came from the depths of his throat.

"Wh-what are you still doing here? I thought you left already?" she asked with a slight tremble in her voice as she fidgeted with her pen.

"We didn't do our walkthrough for the day," he said, still hovering in the doorway.

"Oh, we don't have to today. I trust you."
"Hmm."

Dominic crossed the threshold to fully enter her office, walking slowly towards her desk. His long, lean arms hung at his sides and his abs flexed beneath his shirt with each step. The top two buttons were open, revealing a gold link chain and cross laying against the bronze skin of his toned chest. Leticia studied his every move, just like she did back in the day. His walk always mesmerized her, but it was no match for that thousand watt smile he would flash — just like he was doing now.

"At least one of you do," Dominic commented. "Hey, what's your sister's beef with me, anyway?"
"Please ignore her," Leticia replied, rolling her eyes and waving off any thoughts of Edie.
"Yeah, that's easier said than done," he said with a snort. "But, seriously, what's her deal? Did I do something to her that I don't remember?"
"I mean you did egg her one Halloween," she giggled.
"Well, shit!" he exclaimed with a chuckle.

Leticia explained that her sister has always had a bit of a judgmental attitude towards other people, unfortunately. Especially anyone with any kind of troubled past.

"She doesn't believe people can change," Leticia explained, her chin resting on her fist. '*You are who you are*,' she'd always say."
"And what do you think?" Dominic asked with a furrowed brow.

"I think people have the right to reinvent themselves as many times as they want until they find the version they like. That's what I do," she said, flashing a grin,

Dominic's eyes roamed over Leticia's face, absorbing every single detail. She had pulled her hair up into a messy bun with a few ringlets dangling around her face and purple wide-framed glasses took the place of her contacts. This was the "Tecie" he remembered. The quiet girl who sat in the back of the class, dazed and doodling in her notebooks, but somehow always knew the answer to every question, no matter the subject. That's who he saw each and every time he laid eyes on her, even now, and it always brought back heavy memories. Like the last time he saw her. A moment seared into his mind for the last decade.

Summer '13 - Chicago

Leticia was blowing out the candles on her cake as her family and friends cheered. It was her college graduation/going-away party, and everyone had come together to celebrate. In a week, she would be leaving for New York for a year-long paid internship at a premier interior design company, but Leticia secretly hoped this move would lead to something permanent. For now, she would enjoy spending the afternoon laughing, dancing and opening gifts surrounded by people who loved and would no doubt miss her terribly, but little did she know there was still someone missing...

Dominic had walked by Leticia's house at least eight times already, contemplating whether or not he should pop into the backyard and crash the party. Honestly, all

he really wanted to do was see her. He knew this summer would be different than the last three since graduating high school. This might actually be their last one together, and the thought of that literally made him sick. So much so, that each time Dominic headed towards the backyard, he'd instantly get queasy.

"What the fuck is wrong with me?!" Dominic chastised himself as he paced back and forth on the walkway.
"Well, for starters you're out here talking to yourself," a transient voice called out behind him.

Dominic looked up on the porch and saw it was Leticia's older sister, Edie, scowling down at him. He grunted and shook his head in annoyance at the sight of her. The two of them had never gotten along and Dominic quit trying to figure out what her issue was ages ago. He waved his hand dismissively as he took a deep breath and made his way towards the back gate again.

"Uh, where are you going?!" Edie snapped as she angrily trotted down the porch steps.
"I'm going to the party," Dominic replied dryly, yanking his arm from her grasp when she reached for him.
"Oh no the hell you're not! You weren't invited!" she barked, pulling on the back of his shirt.
"I don't need an invite. It's me!"
"Which is exactly why you can't go back there!"

Edie jumped in front of Dominic, pushing firmly against his chest and halting his steps. He scoffed at the gesture and ordered her to get out of his way, but she adamantly refused.

"Domino, you don't want shit," Edie said firmly. "I've watched you toy with that girl's emotions and take advantage of her for years, and I'm sick of it. This party is for family and friends only. You're neither of those. So, go away!"

"She is my friend, Edie!" Dominic protested, still trying to get by.

"Yeah, but that doesn't mean you're hers. You knew Lettie had a crush on you and milked it for all it was worth. Never gave a damn about her, for real."

Just then, Leticia's face came into view through the crowd as she danced the Samba with one of her uncles. The way her face lit up as she laughed and twirled around almost made tears well up in Dominic's eyes. Edie's words cut him deeply, and it was made worse by the possibility that Tecie thought the same things about him. Suddenly, he felt sick again.

"That's not true, Edie," Dominic pressed. "Tecie has always meant a lot to me, and since I may never see her again, I have to tell her how I feel now."

"Nope, it's too late for that," Edie said flatly, shaking her head. "Leticia is getting away from here and you. If you really felt something for my sister, you should've said it a long time ago. Now, go home, Domino."

Dominic looked down at Edie and then back at a smiling Leticia. She was so happy and had such a bright future ahead of her. Edie was right. He had waited too long. He was too late. For nearly eight years, Dominic had been so used to Leticia always being there, and now he was out of time. He stole one final glance at the sweetest face he'd ever laid eyes on, then sadly turned around to head home...

Dominic always feared he'd never see Leticia again. She always seemed way too good, too kind, too sweet and absolutely too smart to just remain in Chicago forever. She was brilliant, talented and extremely creative. So, it was only right that those attributes would carry her to the moon, and far beyond Dominic's reach. Yet, ten years later, here she was. Leticia Nadal right before his eyes, and well-within his arms' reach. A fact Dominic still found hard to believe, especially now that he was working with her. *What are the odds?* he would often think to himself.

"You'll always be Tecie to me," Dominic said with a light shrug and soft smile.
"And you'll always be *Domino* to me," she said, recalling the comment he'd made to Edie earlier and playfully sticking out her tongue.
"Do you even know why people call me that?" he asked.
"Yeah, because of your birthmark," she replied, tapping her own eye for reference. "But, that's not why I call you that."

Dominic angled his head, looking at her with the most curious eyes. It was true everyone he'd ever known growing up always called him "Domino," because of the faint birthmark around his left eye, and it was also a play on his real name. Not to mention that in sixth grade someone had called him "Patches," and that didn't end so well for them. Dominic had never given much thought to there being any other reason for his nickname, but Leticia's statement had his mind's wheels turning.

"So why *do you* call me Domino?" he inquired in a voice barely above a whisper.
"Because it describes you perfectly," Leticia stated plainly. "No matter how hard you get knocked down, you remain

untarnished and unbroken. Firm, solid and sturdy, just like an actual domino. It's who you are."

The innocent twinkle in her eyes and the sweet smile on her face as she spoke those words made Dominic's insides turn to mush and his knees nearly buckled. Leticia Nadal had always known the direct path to his soul back in the day, just by knowing the right things to say and the perfect time to say them. He was so glad that hadn't changed in all this time.

"You can call me whatever you want," Dominic finally replied in a sultry tone.
"You know, if I were a crazy woman, I'd swear you were flirting with me sometimes," Leticia said with a nervous giggle, trying to hide her reddening cheeks.
"You're not crazy...and you're not wrong," he confirmed with a devious smirk.

Leticia sat erect as the shock of Dominic's words sent chills up her spine. Their eyes locked on each other and a thick silence briefly filled the space between them. She was speechless, but incredibly curious to know exactly what he meant by that statement. After waiting out the pregnant pause, Dominic was the first to cut through the heated tension.

"Well, if there's nothing else you need from me, I guess I'll see you bright and early Monday morning," Dominic said with a soft huff and shrug as he started backing away.
"Uh...yeah, ok. S-see you Monday," Leticia stammered, still reeling.

Dominic stopped short when he reached the doorway and looked at Leticia over his right shoulder. She lifted her brows and tilted her head questioningly – a move that caused a knot to form in Dominic's chest as he gripped the doorjamb tightly.

"I carried a torch for you too, ya know," he said softly, remembering what Edie had revealed about Leticia earlier. "Still do."

With that, he disappeared into the hallway, leaving Leticia with her mouth dropped wide open and head spinning.

Chapter 4

'Twas six days til...

Dominic entered the event site, his heavy boots hitting the floor tiles with fervor and his eyes scanning the room like an Apex predator clocking its prey. He made note of every face he saw milling about, but once again the face he sought out the most was nowhere to be found. He exhaled a dejected sigh and made his way towards the electrical closet.

It had been almost a week since Dominic last saw Leticia face-to-face; since confessing his longtime secret crush, and now he had the distinct feeling she was avoiding him. Had he said too much? Did his words make her too uncomfortable to be around him now? Dominic was a man who prided himself on direct honesty, but maybe he had gone too far. *Damn, I hope not*, he mused to himself as he dropped his work bag to the floor.

The loud clang of the tools inside Dominic's bag made De'Vyne jump, then exhale a sigh of relief, because that was just the man he needed to see.

"Thank God you're here!" De'Vyne exclaimed, flailing his arms as he rushed over to Dominic.

"Good to see you too, D," Dominic replied jokingly as he knelt down and unzipped his tool bag.

"No, you don't understand," De'Vyne said, sounding out of breath. "We have a crisis and I could really use your help."

"*Me*, specifically?"

"The one and only *you*."

Dominic looked up at De'Vyne with a skeptical expression and asked what was the crisis? It turns out there was an error made with the supply company used to order a surplus of Christmas lights for the trees – they didn't send nearly enough lights.

"How many trees do you have and how tall are they?" Dominic asked, rising up from the floor.

"Four and they're all eighteen feet," De'Vyne said in a nervous tone.

"And how many feet of lights do you have?" Dominic inquired as they walked towards the center of the room.

"Eight hundred," De'Vyne replied with a painful grimace.

"*Eight hundred*?! *That's it*?!"

"That's it."

"Yeah, that ain't enough."

Dominic walked up to one of the bare trees, touching the branches to confirm it was artificial. He walked around it, peering between the branches trying to get a good look at the post. He did two laps around the tree before responding to De'Vyne's still unspoken plea for help.

"Y'all have a reimbursement clause in your contract with the city right?" Dominic asked as he scanned the room once again to assess the other three trees.

"For any unexpected expenses incurred? Yeah," De'Vyne confirmed.

"Cool. You got a company card?" Dominic asked, cutting his eyes at him.

"Yeah," De'Vyne replied, raising his brow in suspicion.

"Good. You're gonna need it."

Dominic instructed De'Vyne to go to any nearby hardware store and get at least eight to ten more boxes of Christmas lights, or as many as he could find. He told him he had a plan in mind that should work, but they'd definitely need more strings of lights for it.

"Oh, and tell your team to stop decorating the trees until I get the lights up," Dominic instructed. "I don't wanna knock down or break shit *I* can't pay for."

"Okay. Thank you! Thank you, so much!" De'Vyne exclaimed as he squeezed him tight in a sideways hug.

"Don't thank me yet. This shit might not even work," Dominic said with a chuckle as he went to retrieve his ladder from the electrical closet.

"I'm praying it will," De'Vyne said as he walked away, but stopped short to yell over his shoulder. "Oh, and pleeeaaassseee do not tell Leticia about this. She has enough on her plate right now. This might give her a stroke."

Dominic gave a silent thumbs, as the mere mention of her name made a lump form his throat. When he first arrived at the jobsite, he wondered if she was even there today or working from home again, but now he knew for a fact she was in the building just like him. He quietly hoped for even just a glimpse of her face before he left for the day. They wouldn't even have to talk...he just needed to see her.

As he opened a box of the previously delivered lights and started untangling them, he smiled to himself and made a note to thank De'Vyne for pulling him into this so-called "crisis." Technically, Dominic's job of setting up the power banks and sound systems was nearly complete, and after today, he would have no further reason to be here. Which is why he hoped against hope that Leticia would show her gorgeous face today.

Dominic turned around to grab an extension cord from the utility cart beside him and jumped in surprise at the sight of a stern-faced Edie standing there.

"Where's my sister?" she asked pointedly with her arms folded across her chest.
"What is wrong with you?" Dominic asked in a disgusted tone as he shook his head.
"Excuse me?" she retorted, jerking her head back.
"You're rude as hell for like no reason," he started in an agitated tone. "No 'Good morning,' no 'How are you?' No nothing. Just come in barking orders and demands. What is wrong with you?!"

Dominic huffed and shook his head as he returned to his tasks of propping up the tall ladder and running the extension cord around the base of the tree. He could hear Edie scoffing and murmuring behind him, but resisted the urge to engage, until she decided to provoke him.

"You're demanding respect you don't deserve," Edie stated, her arms still folded. "You are an *em-ploy-ee*. I bark orders, you comply. Period."

"First of all, Edie, fuck you," Dominic exhaled as he rose from the floor, his eyes narrowed. "I don't work for you, and even if I did, there would never be a day where you could talk to me outta the crack of your ass like you do."

"Excuse you?!" she exclaimed, clutching her pearls.

"No, excuse *you*. See, you think you know me, but you don't. You assume, and you know what they say about that."

Edie stepped forward to close the gap between them and drove a stiff finger into his sternum, as she berated him for speaking to her that. She told him she knew all there ever was to know about him and people like him. She said Leticia was a fool for entrusting some two-bit, ex-con to do any work for her, and if she had any say-so about it, he wouldn't have been anywhere near this project.

"You are a menace to society, *Domino*," Edie said, poking him in the chest with each word. "And it doesn't matter how many years have passed or what uniform you put on. That's all you'll ever be."

"You're insane," Dominic said with a smirk. "Is that really what you think about me?"

"It's what I know," she replied in a defiant tone.

"Then you don't know shit. Edie, I've never been to prison a day in my life. Never been to juvie, either. Hell, I've never even been to court for anything other than a traffic ticket."

Dominic told her not only did he not have a prison record, but he had actually gone to college straight out of high school just like everybody else. However, he couldn't afford to finish, so he only did two years. From there, he went to work for his uncle at his auto shop where he learned how to install custom sound systems in cars. Dominic enjoyed the work so much, he decided that's what he wanted to do as a career. His uncle supported his dream and paid for him to go back to school to finish his engineering degree and get his state certification.

"I'm an educated Black man with an honest trade and my own business with a healthy clientele," Dominic continued. "I have a bomb ass resumè, not a prison record. So like I said, you don't know shit about me."

Edie blinked rapidly as she processed Dominic's words. Before she could respond, she heard Leticia's voice behind her and slowly turned away from Dominic to lock eyes with her sister.

"Edie, what are you doing here?" Leticia asked as she walked over to them, purposely avoiding Dominic's gaze.

"Uh...I came to see you," Edie stammered, still trying to recover from her exchange with Dominic. "You haven't been answering my calls or responding to texts. So, I came to check on you."

"I'm fine, Edie," Leticia said dryly, still feeling a little perturbed from their row a few days ago.

Hell yeah, you are, Dominic thought to himself as he watched her out of the corner of his eye. The sight of her smooth, plump calves and the peek-a-boo of fleshy thighs under the hem of her dress made his mouth water. Today was the first time she hadn't worn pants to work, and he could not be more grateful.

Leticia's horchata complexion covered in the dark maroon material was the perfect contrast. The dress stopped at mid-thigh with large pleats and flowed outward, which only accentuated her curvy hips and butt more. The top of the dress hugged her ample bosom, making her breasts sit up higher than she probably intended, but everything about it was perfect in Dominic's eyes.

Begrudgingly, he tore his eyes away from her and started ascending the ladder with the ream of lights draped around his arm — an act that instantly caught her attention.

"Uh, what are you doing?" Leticia asked him, holding up a finger to halt Edie's next words.
"Climbing a tree," Dominic said sarcastically over his shoulder.
"And why are you *climbing a tree*?" she pressed further in her own sarcastic tone.
"Because I was asked to, Tecie."
"By who?"

Just then De'Vyne came rushing back into the room with multiple *Home Depot* bags dangling from his arms and sweat pooling on his forehead. When he spotted Leticia standing there, he murmured a flood of curse words under his breath as he walked towards her.

"H-Hey, Boss Lady," De'Vyne stuttered as he sat the bags down on the floor.
"De'Vyne, what are you up to and why?" Leticia interrogated with her hands on her hips and eyes fixed on her assistant.

De'Vyne exhaled a heavy sigh and told her about the fiasco with the Christmas lights. The more he talked, the wider her eyes got and the louder her, "What?!" became. As she started to fuss and curse in Spanish with her arms flailing in the air, De'Vyne tried to reassure her that there was a perfectly good solution in the works.

"What possible solution could there be that won't make this a shitshow in six days?!" Leticia exclaimed angrily.

"This," De'Vyne said cheerfully as he pulled a box of lights from one of the bags.

"How does that help me, De'Vyne?!" she demanded.

"It doesn't," Dominic interrupted as he reached past her to take the box and look it over. "It helps me."

Dominic explained that he and De'Vyne have a plan and that Leticia could rest assured nothing else would or could go wrong — at least not with the Christmas trees.

"Dominic, this isn't your problem," Leticia said with an exasperated breath.

"It's a lighting problem. I'm the lighting guy. Thus, it's my problem," Dominic said matter-of-factly.

"But, you didn't come here to be bothered with Christmas trees," she groaned.

"I came here to help you. Let me help you, Tecie," he replied softly with the twinkle of a smile in his eyes.

"I...okay," she relented.

Leticia, Edie and De'Vyne walked away to let Dominic get on with his plan to remedy the lights situation, and as she went he watched the sway of her hips with every step. Leticia could feel the heat of his gaze caressing her waistline and it made her spine go rigid as she stole a glance at him on the way out of the room. Their eyes met briefly, and he didn't even bother to avert or pretend as if he wasn't watching her.

He just threw her a wink which made her face immediately flush red before she disappeared out of sight.

Several hours later, Dominic was packing up his work bag when he heard steps approaching behind him. He looked over his shoulder and saw De'Vyne breezing towards him with a smile on his face.

"Aye, man, you all out of favors for the day," Dominic tossed over his shoulder as he hoisted his bag up off the ground.

"Ha! That's not even why I'm here," De'Vyne laughed as he brought his hand from behind his back and passed him a pristine white envelope.

"What's that?" Dominic asked with a furrowed brow.

"It's an official invite to the Christmas party next Friday," De'Vyne said gleefully.

He told Dominic how grateful he was for all his help with the Christmas lights earlier and how much of a relief it was to Leticia, as well. The whole team appreciated all of his hard work and always having the perfect solution to any problem right in his back pocket over the past two weeks.

"I know you came here just to work on sound and lights, but you did so much more for us and we just wanted to thank you for it," De'Vyne explained as he happily clasped his hands together in front of him.

"Damn, thank you, man," Dominic said graciously with a wide smile. "Y'all didn't have to do this, but I really appreciate it."

"You deserve it."

"Thanks."

The two of them shook hands and Dominic headed out. When the doors opened to one of the elevator cars, he saw Leticia standing there bathed in the warm fluorescent lighting inside. She stared at him with a longing she was too afraid to express, and parted her lips to say words she ached to say, but nothing came out. So, she smiled awkwardly and stepped off the elevator, brushing past him. The scent of her sweet perfume invaded his senses, making him moan low in his throat.

"Oh, wait,"Leticia called out to him. "Tonight's your last night, right?"

"Yeah, you're officially rid of me," Dominic replied with a slight smirk.

"Don't say it like that," she said with a giggle. "But, thank you so much for everything. Literally could not have done this without you."

"That's nice of you to say. Glad I could be of service," he said in a low voice.

The depth of his raspy baritone snaked its way through her ears and worked its way through her torso, settling in her core and making her cross her legs at the ankles and pinch her thighs together. Trying to maintain her self-control, Leticia switched gears and asked if he'd received his invitation. When he said he had, she told him how much she looked forward to seeing him in his masquerade costume next week.

"You could see me sooner, if you're interested," Dominic said in a hopeful tone.

"What do you mean?" Leticia asked with a shaky voice, her legs still locked together.

"Go on a date with me, Tecie," he said pointedly.

"A what?" her voice barely above a whisper.

"A date. You know, dinner? A movie? Ice skating at *Maggie Daley Park*? A date."

For what felt like an eternity, Leticia stood there in stunned silence, exhaling one trembling breath after another. Dominic held her gaze captive as he waited with his own baited breath for her answer. He took a step forward to be closer to her, to emphasize the seriousness of his request and his need to hear her say "Yes." Leticia's eyes fluttered closed as Dominic's body heat washed over her from his closeness.

She inhaled a deep breath when she felt Dominic brush a wisp of hair from her forehead. The spice and musk of his cologne penetrated her nose and made her whole body tingle. Pressing her thighs together was no longer working, and her knees immediately felt weak when Dominic whispered her name to get her to look at him.

Her eyelids flew open and she was immediately met with the pleading that lay in Dominic's brown eyes. So badly, she wanted to cup his face in her hands. To pull his perfect blush pink lips to hers and finally know what they taste like. To feel his strong hands clutching her waist again like they did on that first day. So badly, she wanted so much...but she knew she couldn't have it.

"I can't," Leticia said simply, almost sounding remorseful.

"You can't? Dominic asked, trying to understand.

"I can't," she repeated softly, her eyes begging him not to make her explain further.

"Because we work together, right? I get it," he replied quietly with a nod.

Dominic leaned forward and pressed his lips to her left cheek, letting them linger for a moment. As he pulled away, he whispered, "Goodbye, Leticia," and walked backwards to the elevator. The sound of her name on his lips attached to a "Goodbye" caused a painful sting in her heart. It had been over a decade since they'd last seen each other and who knows if or when they'd ever see each other again.

As the doors closed, Leticia's bottom lip began to quiver as she blinked back tears. She shook her head, trying to dispel the emotions bubbling up inside her. Not being able to stand the sight of the numbers above the elevator tick backwards any longer, Leticia quickly spun on her heels and headed towards the event space to do her nightly walkthrough before going home.

The moment Leticia stepped into the room, her hands flew to her mouth. The four green trees were fully decorated with various ornaments, candy canes; gold, silver, red and green foil tinsel draped across the branches. The glass ornaments and baubles flickered and danced in the light, instantly drawing attention to them. There were miniature masquerade masks adorning two of the trees, giving them a bit of a Mardi Gras aesthetic, just like the theme of the party. Atop each tree was a Swarovski crystal star that flashed iridescent, but what really made Leticia's heart swell was the lighting.

Dominic had wrapped the posts of the trees in strands of multicolored lights. There was a remote attached with a control dial he had set to "Dancing," which made the lights blink to their own rhythm. They illuminated the trees from the inside out and from the very top all the way to the base. The issue of not having enough lights earlier was now non-existent.

Leticia's eyes welled up with tears once again as she squealed in excitement. At that moment, she truly saw the fruits of her labor coming together, and started to believe that this party would go exactly as planned. She rushed into De'Vyne's arms and they squeezed each other tight as they celebrated closing in on the finish line of this project.

"This looks amazing!" Leticia squealed as she went up to one of the trees, gingerly touching the ornaments.
"That man is a miracle worker! Because I did not expect this," De'Vyne exclaimed as he peered between the branches at the dancing lights.
"That he is," she agreed in a hushed tone.
"So, you still playing hard-to-get or nah?" he asked, cutting his eyes at her and smirking.
"Am I what?!"
"Oh, Miss Ma'am, even a blind man can see the fireworks between y'all two. Now, I know you got that weird rule about not dating people you work with, buuuuttt now he's not working with you anymore. Soooo...?"

Leticia slowly pulled her hand away from the tree and dropped her eyes to the floor at De'Vyne's question. The slump in her shoulders made him concerned and he asked if everything was okay, but when she revealed Dominic had asked her out and she said "No," he let her have it.

"You what?!" De'Vyne exclaimed. "Why?!"

"Because in what world do I actually get a guy like that?" Leticia asked, her voice cracking.

"In this one!" he said plainly. "That man *wants* you. Even *I* know that. And now, so do you. Call him, tell him you're full of shit and you're sorry. Then say yes."

"I can't, Dev. I just can't," she said, shaking her head.

"You can. You're just scared. My question is why, though?"

As they walked back to her office, Leticia told De'Vyne of her history with Dominic. Their years at Jefferson High School, always having at least one class together every semester for four years straight. Living on the same block for years, and seeing him shirtless all summer as he roamed their street every day. She had the biggest crush on him, and tried so hard not to be obvious about it, but knew she failed miserably every day.

Leticia would blush and giggle like a maniac everytime Dominic even spoke to her, and Edie would get so mad at her for it. "He's just a boy! Get yourself together!" she'd yell constantly. The embarrassment Leticia felt when her sister said that was nothing compared to the pain she'd feel seeing Dominic with other girls around the neighborhood; but it was always soothed by the fact that no matter who he was with or what he was doing, he made it a point to speak to her. Whether in class or sitting on her front porch, Dominic Ballantyne was guaranteed to say, "Tecie Boo! What it do?!" each and every time.

She told De'Vyne that even though Dominic was what some may consider popular in high school with a bit of a bad boy edge, he was always sweet to her. He defended her when other people teased her. Whenever he saw her sitting alone, he'd come over and join her. Dominic would come to her first when he needed help with homework, and she always laughed at how excited he got seeing her after her Food & Nutrition class because he knew she was coming with snacks. He even told her one day, "I hope you know, you've spoiled me, and you're stuck with me," when she had made him peanut butter cookies.

"Sounds to me like he was putting his bid in even back then," De'Vyne said with a side-eye.

"No, he was just being nice to the nerdy, fluffy girl," Leticia said with a dejected shrug.

"Boss Lady, I mean this with all my love and respect," he started. "But, you're still nerdy and *fabulously* fluffy."

"Well, gee, thanks," she replied gruffly, rolling her eyes.

"No, hear me out. You are gorgeous with cheekbones I'd kill for. The *girls* be sittin' and the booty be poppin', honey! You got body-on-body that's soft, supple and plush in all the best places. Big legs, full lips and luxurious hair. You always give 'naughty librarian' mixed with 'shy virgin energy,' that would drive any man crazy. And *that man* wants you, in every way! Trust me."

De'Vyne encouraged Leticia once again to give Dominic a call and a chance, because he deserves and so does she. Leticia pondered on his words, still feeling unsure.

Does Dominic really like me like that? Or is he just a man who likes to flirt? But, why would he ask you out if he wasn't for real? Eh, maybe he was just being nice like always. Her thoughts funneled through her mind like water swirling down the drain.

The confusion and uncertainty of a man's true feelings and intentions were one of the main reasons why Leticia hated the dating scene and just hurled herself into her work. Now, the lines between those two worlds were blurred with the arrival of Dominic Ballantyne, and she was more confused than ever.

Before leaving for the day, De'Vyne offered one final urging to his boss to give Dominic a call, because he was certain the man's intentions were genuine. Leticia ruminated on De'Vyne's advice, but still couldn't shake the doubts she had. Then as she reached the doorway of her office and flicked off the lights, suddenly Dominic's voice echoed in her head from a very particular day.

"I carried a torch for you too. Still do."

Leticia's eyes widened as that realization set in. *Domino wants me?!* she thought to herself. *Carried a torch for me?! Asked me on a date and I said "No?!"*

"The fuck is wrong with me?!" she chastised herself as she pulled her cellphone from her purse and scrolled until she found Dominic's number.

Chapter 5

'Twas the night of...

De'Vyne handed Leticia the mirror to assess her makeup as he adjusted the straps of her dress and secured the zipper. She donned a royal blue satin, off-the-shoulder gown with corset bodice and mermaid skirt. Her hair was pulled up in a faux-hawk with rhinestones pinned throughout.

Leticia smiled with joy at De'Vyne's handiwork. Her eyeshadow was a smokey blend of silver, black and blue with full lashes and glittery eyeliner on her lower lid. Pink-tinted nude lipstick with brown lipliner created an ombre hue on her lips, and blush was lightly brushed across her cheekbones.

"This looks amazing! Thank you!" she gushed while leaning on his shoulder as he helped with her shoes.
"I had to make sure my girl looked *phenom* on her big night!" De'Vyne replied with a wink.
"And so do you," she complimented.
"Well, you know," he said with the click of his tongue as he dragged the pad of his middle finger across his perfectly arched eyebrow.

De'Vyne wore a metallic silver shirt with a large bow collar and bell sleeves, black slim-fit slacks and silver *Christian Louboutin* loafers. His makeup was just as bold with feathery lash extensions and glitter adorning his cheekbones. The two of them looked exquisite for tonight's festivities.

The Mayor's Christmas Masquerade Party to benefit the City Colleges of Chicago and Chicago Public Schools had finally arrived and Leticia could not be more excited. Over the last two weeks, she was sure she'd lose her mind trying to pull this off, but tonight her very own Christmas miracle was coming to fruition.

Leticia picked up her blue mask with gold and silver glitter and feathered adornments from her desk, hooked her arm in De'Vyne's and they headed upstairs to the enclosed rooftop. Music vibrated through the hallway as they stepped off the elevator and rounded the corner to see attendees mingling just outside the room.

The room was full of partygoers, some in masks and some just in dramatic makeup, dressed to the nines and imbibing on the open bar and floating trays of champagne. There were aerial dancers suspended from the rafters, spinning and twirling to the musical stylings of the DJ across the room.

The Christmas trees illuminated the four corners of the room beautifully, and no one would ever know the secret of making that happen. Leticia spotted Edie and Hector and separated from De'Vyne to go greet them.

"There she is!" her brother-in-law, Hector, cheered in Spanish when he spotted her.

"Hey, Bro!" Leticia said excitedly back in Spanish as they hugged tightly.

"This looks amazing! I knew you could pull it off," he praised.

"Whew! It definitely was an experience," she exhaled heavily with a laugh.

"Congrats, Lettie. You did a wonderful job," Edie chimed in from beside her husband.

Leticia eyed her sister suspiciously at first, unsure if her praises were genuine or not, but the proud smile on her face was confirmation enough. The sisters embraced each other, rocking side-to-side gleefully. Hector took Leticia around to introduce and brag about her to some of the premier guests in attendance, namely the Mayor and a slew of Commissioners and Directors for the city.

Her head was spinning, face hurting from smiling and eyes struggling to readjust after a barrage of cameras flashing in her face for the last hour. Leticia was finally able to break away from the crowd and get to the bar, where she spotted De'Vyne stirring his martini.

"The woman of the hour! You look like you need a drink," he chuckled.

"You have no idea!" she laughed back as she ordered a cranberry and vodka cocktail.

When her drink arrived, the two of them clinked their glasses to another successful Leticia Nadal Production. They watched the crowd dance and revel in the festive entertainment provided for the night. Just as De'Vyne spotted Edie and Hector dancing together, a thought occurred to him.

"So, where's mister man this evening?" he asked, referring to Dominic.

"Probably not coming since I blew it with him," Leticia said dejectedly as she polished off her drink and ordered a refill.

"What do you mean?" he asked, raising a dramatic eyebrow.

"Because I never called after turning down his date invite," she revealed and quickly kept talking, preventing De'Vyne from laying into her. "I chickened out that night, and every day after that. I just kept making excuses not to call him. Now here we are a week later, and I *still* haven't called."

"Guess that explains the no RSVP."

"Yup."

Like De'Vyne, Leticia had been watching the event queue to see if Dominic would officially accept their party invite and RSVP, even though she rejected his date request. Secretly, she hoped he would at least show up so she could apologize for being such a chicken before and ask him out instead. She found herself watching the door every time someone new walked in, and instantly felt the pain of disappointment at it not being him.

"Yeah, so, Merry, Merry or whatever," Leticia sighed sarcastically as she downed her second drink.

"I still think you should call him, or at least text," De'Vyne suggested, giving her a side-eye.

"Nah, it's too late for that," she replied, sounding sad.

"It's never too late to go for what you want, Ma'am, and that includes a fine ass man," he punctuated his statement with a playful hip bump before sashaying away into the crowd to dance with someone that had piqued his own interest.

Leticia laughed lightly at his last words, but pondered on the weight of them. Could De'Vyne be right about there still being a chance with Dominic? Or was the sting of her rejection too much to recover from? There was only one way to find out. She pushed off from the bar, whizzing through the throng of attendees to head out the door, but bumped into her sister.

"Where's the fire?" Edie asked playfully in Spanish.

"Girl, you know how surgically attached I am to my cell phone," Leticia replied jokingly. "I feel so naked right now. I'm just running down to my office. I'll be right back."

"Okay, but don't be gone too long. Hector has a surprise for you," Edie hinted with a wink.

"Ooohh! Well, let me hurry up!" Leticia squealed as she dashed into the hallway.

Leticia made it to the elevators just as the doors opened and a crowd exited heading to the party. She spoke to a few people she recognized and waited for everyone to get off before she got on. Just as the crowd dissipated, one lone passenger remained, standing at the back, leaning against the wall with his hands in his pockets.

It was something in the way he looked at her, even through his black and silver half-mask, that set Leticia's skin on fire. She knew exactly who it was.

She stared in awe at Dominic Ballantyne, who stood there just as cool and calm as ever, draped in a midnight blue suit that shimmered in the elevator lighting. The dark color against his golden skin was immaculate. His neatly trimmed beard framed perfect lips that curled into a subtle smirk as his eyes swept over Leticia's body, from top to bottom and back again.

"Aren't you going to the party?" Leticia asked nervously, trying to steady her breathing and pointing towards the hall.

"I go where you go," Dominic said, his voice low, husky and caressing every inch of her ear.

Leticia softly gasped at the directness of his statement and tried, but to no avail, hiding her smile as she stepped on the elevator. She could feel the heat of his eyes on the bare skin of her back that was visible through her dress. It was so intense, it might as well have just been his actual hands – not that she would mind if it was. They took the elevator ride in silence, enveloped in thick tension and pheromones.

They departed at the thirty-fourth floor, with Dominic leisurely following behind Leticia, watching the sway of her hips. His hands were still in his pockets and his loafers clicked along the tiles, matching each step she took. The echoes were the only sounds made until they reached her office.

"I didn't think I'd see you tonight," Leticia finally said, breaking through the silence as she walked over to her desk.

"Why? You invited me, remember?" Dominic inquired as he closed the door and leaned against it.

"Yeah, but you never RSVP'd. So, I thought you weren't coming," she said over her shoulder.

"Ah...well, you know how much I hate following rules," he answered, smiling coyly.

Leticia giggled at the memory of their high school days and all the times she witnessed him getting in trouble for defying one rule or another without any remorse or regret.

"Yeah, you did have a little problem with authority," Leticia teased. "I don't know how you survived working for me these last few weeks."

"I'd gladly let you boss me around anytime you want," Dominic said plainly, his eyes piercing her soul.

Leticia inhaled sharply once again, her lungs stinging and reminding her to breathe. She dropped her eyes to the desk, spotting her cell phone, which was the only reason she was down there anyway. It would be so easy to just grab it and go back to the party, but she'd wanted this moment alone with Dominic for nearly a week.

"Domino, I owe you an explanation," she began.

"For?" Dominic asked, a slight frown marring his features as he pulled off his mask.

"For turning you down last week," she said softly.

"Nah, you don't have to explain your 'No' to me. I respect it," he replied with a light shrug, driving his hands back into his pockets and adjusting his posture against the door.

"You probably won't after I tell you why I said it," she said quietly.

Leticia walked around her desk, coming to stand in the middle of the floor. She removed her own mask, so he could fully see the sincerity in her eyes as she explained her hesitancy to respond to his advances. She confessed her uncertainty, and maybe even a bit of insecurity where Dominic was concerned.

"I never know if you're flirting because you're just being nice or toying with me," Leticia admitted as she fidgeted with the strings of her mask in her hands.

"Why would I be toying with you?" Dominic asked, narrowing his eyes.

"I don't know *why* you would, but I guess it's the same as when we were kids," she said. "You used to act all cute and flirty with me back then, too, but I knew you weren't serious. I just thought you were being nice...or maybe just playing a joke."

Dominic turned his head to look away from her, trying to process what she'd just said. No matter how many times he'd imagined this scenario and conversation, he never saw it going this way. Her words pierced his eardrums and his heart, because Leticia really thought there was no way he'd genuinely flirt with or be interested in her. The realization of that was more painful than Dominic could've ever imagined.

His silence was deafening to Leticia and suddenly she felt awkward and way too exposed by her confession that he'd yet to respond to. Especially with him not even bothering to look her in the eyes right now. She couldn't take it anymore and immediately regretted the entire exchange. Leticia dropped her arms in embarrassed defeat and walked to the door, attempting to push past Dominic and reach for the doorknob. What happened next was the last thing she ever expected.

Dominic snaked his arm under Leticia's and slowly moved it up her body until his palm came to rest against her throat. Gently squeezing the pulse on each side of her neck as he caressed the side of her face with his breath. When Leticia felt his soft lips on the skin of her neck just along her hairline, she let out a soft whimper. Her forehead and palms were pressed to the door and knees locked together the second she felt that familiar pulsing between her legs.

With Dominic's hard body pinned to her back and pelvis pushing into her soft ass, Leticia was literally between a rock and a hard place, and right now she couldn't tell which was which. The wetness of Dominic's tongue trailing along the space between her neck and collarbone was such a sensual shock to her system that she moaned his name loudly before she could stop herself.

"Dominic..." his real name slid across her lips like a cool ice cube.

"Mmmm...Yes, Le-ti-ci-a?" Dominic growled hers just as ravenously as he felt, elongating every syllable.

He inhaled the scent of her hair – hibiscus and strawberries – and became hypnotized by the woman wedged between him and the office door. He sank so easily into her soft body, that he could only imagine what it would feel like to become completely lost in her.

Leticia moaned again as she felt Dominic's erection grow harder, pressing firmly into her ass. Having a mind of their own, her hips began grinding against him, making Dominic tighten his grip around her throat as he released a feral groan of his own into her ear. She knew if they didn't stop now, they'd reach the point of no return, and she couldn't allow that to happen. Not here. Not with him.

Leticia pushed off the door and turned around to face Dominic. Now that they were face-to-face, she nearly lost her nerve. Especially, once he placed his palms at either side of her head on the door. His face hovered over hers and he absorbed everything she was in that moment. The dark brown of her eyes and how they contrast to her smooth vanilla skin. The rounded fullness of her face that he always wanted to trace with his finger, right down to the rise and fall of her plump breasts as she took one quickened, nervous breath after another.

Dominic leaned forward, touching the tip of his nose to hers, but before his lips could follow suit, he felt her small hand collide into his chest. He looked down at it, then back to her eyes, tilting his head in confusion. Leticia slipped under his right arm and walked away from him on wobbly legs. She stopped short in front of her desk and spun on her heels when she heard footsteps coming up behind her.

"Stop!" Leticia said firmly with her arm outstretched.
"Did I do something wrong?" Dominic asked, stopping so abruptly that his shoes squeaked across the floor tile.
"This," she said, shaking her head. "This can't happen."
"Why not?" he asked, trying to hide a smirk. "Because we're at work?"
"Because it's not real!"

Dominic's posture went rigid, eyes narrowed and lips pursed at Leticia's words. He shoved his hands back into his pockets and watched her in stoic silence for a moment – partly pondering on what she had said and partly to see if she'd say more. Now it was her muteness that screamed at infinite volumes.

"Why is it so hard for you to believe how I feel about you?" Dominic asked after a while, his voice firm and direct.
"*Maybe* because I don't know how you actually feel about me," Leticia retorted in a snappy tone.
"I *feel* like you're the most beautiful woman I've ever known, and I don't just mean physically," he started. "You are sweet and way too caring about people who don't deserve an

ounce of your kindness. I've honestly always thought that, even back in high school."

Leticia watched closely as Dominic took a step forward, being sure to keep his movements slow and calculated.

"I *feel* like your smile has always been my favorite feature," Dominic continued. "Next one is your eyes, because of how you see me when no one else ever has."

Leticia sat on the edge of her desk and listened intently to his every word, clinging to the desire to believe each one of them. Her heart started racing again, like it did when their bodies were fused together at her office door. This time he had her pinned in place by his vulnerability and blunt honesty – a welcomed pressure she'd gladly fall under.

"I *feel* that this newfound confidence you have is so fucking sexy," Dominic admitted. "Honestly, it's just an extension of the sexiness I've always felt you had. It makes it damn near impossible to be around you every day because it's so hard not to touch you. Probably the hardest thing I've ever had to deal with in my life."

Dominic walked forward some more, closing the gap between them and finally being back within arm's reach.

"I want you, Leticia Nadal. All of you," he stated plainly. "That's how I feel about you. Now you know."

He watched closely as Leticia's body relaxed and she exhaled a heavy sigh. Her eyes fluttered quickly as the gravity of his words settled in her mind. Leticia repeatedly parted her lips to speak, but nothing would come out. Dominic's eyes were fixed on her like a cheetah eyeing its prey – intense, focused and unwavering.

Searching her eyes for an answer to the question that lay in his own, Dominic slowly licked his lips and felt a jolt in his loins when he saw her do the same. He leaned in close, brushing his coarse beard against her cheek as he inhaled the heady scent along her neck and moaning softly near her ear when he felt her hands slip inside his suit jacket and grip his ribs.

"I want to kiss you so bad, but I don't wanna mess up your lipstick," Dominic whispered, looking deep into her eyes.
"It's smudge proof," Leticia whispered back with a smile tugging at her lips.
"Oh, thank God!" he softly exclaimed as he cupped her face in his hands and captured her mouth with his own.

The fleshiness of their lips joined together, as his tongue massaged hers and their breathing grew heavier. Dominic kissed Leticia with all the longing he'd ached with for over a decade. He always wondered what it would be like to kiss her, and now that he was, nothing could make him stop. Leticia's small hands caressed his torso so tenderly as she finally allowed herself to succumb to the wilds of Dominic Ballantyne, but for her, kissing wasn't enough.

Leticia traced Dominic's lips with her tongue, then captured his bottom lip between her teeth. He groaned with pleasure as he slid his hand from her face and gripped her throat again, a move that made her smile sinisterly. He turned her head slightly to give himself full access to the left side of her neck, and he began drawing circles along her pulse with the tip of his tongue. Her grip on him tightened and the throbbing in her core intensified. Panting in ecstasy and her eyes full of fire and passion, Leticia needed more.

"Make love to me," she demanded in a breathy whisper against his ear.

"Mmm, I'd love to, baby," Dominic moaned against her neck. "But, you have a party to get back to."

"So?!" she retorted in a high pitched voice, her eyes darting around in confusion.

"So, me making love to you requires I leave no part of your body untouched," he explained slowly. "That I discover all the different ways to make you cum over…and over…and over. And you don't have that kinda time. Not right now, anyway."

Dominic smirked and brushed his knuckles along her cheek and jawline as he spoke – a combination that only made her want him more. His voice made her blood run hot like lava coursing through her veins, and she could no longer press her knees and thighs together to ward off the horniness she felt.

"Maybe not," Leticia began. "But, you do have time to fuck me."

"What?" Dominic asked abruptly, his smile fading and hand freezing in midair.

"Fuck…Me…Domino," she commanded as she leaned in closer with each word until her breast were pressed against his abs.

Dominic's smile returned and his eyes darkened as he gripped the back of her head and covered her mouth with his once again, this time with much more hunger and ferocity. He told her she could boss him around anytime, and he meant it.

It was at this very moment he realized just how much of a turn on it was.

"Yes, ma'am," he said seductively against her lips.

He undid the single button on his jacket and Leticia pushed the material off his shoulders and down his arms, tossing it on the chair next to them. Dominic pulled Leticia to her feet and turned her around. He kissed the top of her spine and shoulder blades as he eased down the zipper of her dress and pushed the straps down her arms until it became a pool of satin at her feet. He picked it up and tossed it in the chair with his jacket.

Leticia stood there in a black lace one-piece body shaper that accentuated her curves. Dominic's hands caressed the skin of her hips, ass and thighs as he nipped at the sensitive area at the back of her neck. Leticia bit her bottom lip as the feel of his hands on her body aroused her to the highest level. She turned around to face him and started unbuttoning his shirt while he bent down to kiss and caress her cleavage. Dominic hooked his fingers through the straps of the body shaper and started pulling them down, until Leticia stopped him.

"It actually has snaps," she said, pointing down between her legs.

"Merry Christmas to me," Dominic replied with a devilish grin, his voice deep and sultry.

He pulled out the other empty chair beside them, turned Leticia towards it and instructed her to put her knees in the seat, which she did happily. As she did, Dominic spotted a spool of red tinsel on her desk and got an idea. He encircled his arm around her waist and pressed his lips close to her ear.

"You still trust me, right?" he asked, stroking her arm with the knuckles of his free hand.

"Yes, I trust you," Leticia said with a shaky breath.

Dominic tilted her head back and kissed her deeply as he slid his hand from around her waist to between her legs. Finding the snaps of her one-piece, he popped them open in one smooth motion and slipped his middle finger through the opening, sliding it along the slit of her lips until they parted. The second she felt his finger rub against her clit, Leticia's back arched and she let out a throaty moan. Dominic drew circles along her clit with the pad of his finger while cupping her breasts with his other hand, holding her close as he touched and teased her.

Leticia's body jerked and she grabbed his arm tightly, signaling that she just orgasmed because of him for the very first time. The knowledge of that made Dominic insanely hard and he could no longer resist being inside of her. He released his hold on her and grabbed the tinsel he had spotted. Coming around the chair to stand in front of her, he unraveled the tinsel and smiled as her eyes widened with the realization of what he had planned.

Dominic kissed her once more, wrapped the tinsel one time around each of her wrists and then tied the ends around the back legs of the chair; leaving Leticia leaned over the back of the chair with her ass in the air and spine perfectly arched. She giggled the entire time at how excited he was to tie her up with Christmas tree tinsel, of all things.

When he finished tying her up, he went to stand behind her. After a short while of nothing happening, Leticia asked if everything was alright and he told her he was just enjoying the view. She giggled again, making her plump ass jiggle slightly and it drove him wild. Dominic slapped her cheeks with both hands, biting his lip and moaning each time he did. Then he pulled down his pants and boxers, pushed back the open flaps of his shirt and moved closer to Leticia until his hard erection teased at the opening of her wet pussy.

"What do you want me to do again?" Dominic asked slyly as he continued rubbing his dick against her lips and clit.

"Mmm...fuck me, Domino," she moaned as she wiggled her hips and ass against him.

"Gladly," he moaned in return as he slid inside of her with ease – like he belonged there.

The second he felt the wetness and warmth of her flesh wrapped around him, Dominic took in a long sip of air and gripped her hips fiercely. He wasn't ready for it to feel like this. He'd admit there had been fantasies and imaginings, but now that he was in it, he was fighting like hell to stay in it. The recoil of her hips and ass from every thrusts he gave, the way her walls clenched around him, the sound of their skin slapping together echoing throughout the office – all of it sent Dominic's heart racing and blood boiling.

Leticia pressed her face into the cushion of the chairback to muffle her screams of pleasure as Dominic moved in and out of her core, pushing her further over the edge each time he entered. The curve of his dick hit her G-Spot dead center on every thrust, and Leticia lost count of how many times she had cum. Her toes curled tightly inside her stilettos as Dominic worked her body.

Between the feel of his thick dick in her pussy and her being restricted by the makeshift bondage, her orgasms were more intense than she'd ever known before. She released a scream from deep within her chest as another surge rushed through her body. Dominic dug his nails into her lush flesh as he felt the knot forming low in his abdomen, signaling he was close to losing it. Sweat poured down his chest and pooled around his pelvis as it slapped against her skin over and over. The heat of their passion was everything he thought it would be and then some.

"Fuck, Tecie!" Dominic grunted loudly and thrusted harder. "I *knew* you had some good ass pussy!"

"Oh...my...fucking...God!" Leticia cried with each thrust as she gripped the legs of the chair tightly and gave over to another shattering orgasm.

The sensation of her walls clenching his manhood again was the last straw. Dominic sped up his movements, pushing harder and faster until he found his own release – exhaling a barrage of curse words each time his body spasmed in ecstasy. He collapsed forward, his head falling right in the center of Leticia's back. They both fell into a euphoric laughing fit as they rode out the last of their sexual high.

"Perfect! No one will ever know I ravaged you," Dominic said playfully as he adjusted the straps of her dress.

"Yeah, but they may know about me ravaging you," Leticia joked as she tried smoothing out the wrinkles in his shirt.

"Oh, I don't give a damn!" he exclaimed with a wide smile.

She shook her head laughing and made one last check of her dress. Seeing no signs of wear – or at least none that would be hard to explain – she picked up her mask, and cell phone that she had originally come upstairs for, and headed towards the door with Dominic. He was slipping his jacket back on, watching her intently. For a moment, they just held each other's gaze, feeling no need for words. Then Dominic grabbed Leticia by the waist, cuffed her chin with his finger and gently kissed her lips.

"Hi," he said against her mouth, his voice deep and sensual.
"Hey, Papi," Leticia greeted back, her voice low and raspy from screaming.
"Mmm, say that again," he demanded, still hovering over her lips
"Hey, Papi," she repeated with a smile.

Dominic released another guttural groan as he sealed the moment with another kiss. Leticia could feel herself glowing as she pulled open the door to head towards the elevators. Just before she crossed the threshold into the hallway, she turned to face Dominic again, who furrowed his brow questioningly.

"Thank you for coming tonight," she said sweetly with a joyful twinkle in her eye.
"Baby, I'd *cum* for you any night," Dominic replied with a sneaky grin.
"Oh, my God!" she huffed with a laugh as her face went red.
Dominic gave her ass a firm pat as he closed the door behind them.

Chapter 6

'Twas a fairy tale ending...

Leticia and Dominic exited the elevator arm-in-arm and glowing brighter than the tree in Daley Plaza. Coy, covert smiles across their faces and infinite secrets in their eyes hidden behind masks. Leticia's core still throbbed and tingled with the memory of Dominic slipping in and out of her walls – etching his name on every inch as he went.

Suddenly, her skin flushed warm when she looked down at her wrists and saw the faint indents the tinsel had left behind. She giggled quietly to herself, making Dominic ask what was so funny? Before she could answer, De'Vyne came rushing towards them as they crossed the threshold back into the Christmas party.

"There you are!" De'Vyne squealed, his arms flailing frantically. "Oh! Dominic, you came?"
"Yeah, I did," Dominic replied, a Cheshire grin spreading across his face.

Leticia softly elbowed Dominic in his side for the double entendre, while biting the inside of her lip to keep from smiling right along with him.

"Here I am! Where's the crisis?" Leticia asked her assistant, getting back to the task at hand.

"They've been looking for you," De'Vyne informed her. "You're needed on stage."

Without another word, he pried Leticia from Dominic's grasp and whisked her away towards the stage at the front of the room between one of the giant Christmas trees and the DJ booth. Dominic chuckled and shook his head as he followed the duo through to the crowd just to see where they were running off to. As he threaded through fellow onlookers, he heard a booming voice coming through the sound system he had so expertly installed.

"Here she is, ladies and gentlemen! The true star of the show!" Hector announced loudly and proudly into the microphone.

De'Vyne held Leticia's hand as she gingerly mounted the short staircase up to the stage. She walked towards her brother-in-law, who was standing with his arm outstretched to greet her happily.

"This amazing, extravagant affair was the brainchild of this extremely talented woman, right here," Hector continued. "Let's hear a round of applause for Thee Leticia Nadal!"

The crowd of partygoers erupted with cheers, jeers and rousing applause, making Leticia smile and blush nervously. She playfully curtsied and mouthed words of gratitude as the crowd cheerfully roared. Hector continued to speak once the ruckus died down.

"Leticia took on this immense challenge and exceeded even her own expectations, of which we could not be prouder," he complimented. "On behalf of the Mayor's office, but mostly myself, I'd like to present you with a small token of appreciation."

Hector's assistant mounted the stage carrying a framed certificate, small wooden plaque and a white envelope. As everyone waited with bated breaths, Dominic stared at a beaming Leticia in pure awe. The bright spot light shining down on her like a light from heaven...like the angel she was.

His trance was interrupted by the harsh sound of someone clearing their throat very close to his ear. Dominic abruptly turned to his right and saw Edie's scowling face mere inches from his own.

"The fuck?!" he exclaimed, jerking his head backwards. "Hi, Edie."
"What are you doing here, Domino?" she immediately inquired, skipping all pleasantries.
"I was invited, same as you," he replied dryly, turning his attention back to the stage.
"I don't believe that."
"Yeah, and I don't care."

Dominic dismissively shrugged his shoulders as he shifted his mask from eyes up to his forehead so his view of Leticia could be unobstructed. He was trying his best to pay attention, but Edie wouldn't leave well-enough alone.

"Look, I don't know what your fascination is with toying with my sister's feelings, but..." Edie pressed, but was quickly cut off.

"I'm not toying with her feelings, Edie," Dominic contested. "Despite what you've convinced yourself of about me, I actually care about Tecie. She means a lot to me."

"Oh yeah, and after all these years have you finally found the balls to tell her that?" she asked sarcastically.

"Yeah, I did."

"And how'd she take it?"

The air of skepticism in Edie's tone irritated Dominic, but the flashes of Leticia's fat ass and echoes of her passionate cries quickly invaded his mind. He exhaled a throaty laugh and smirked right before answering Edie's question.

"Like a champ, actually," Dominic said coyly before nodding and walking away, leaving a confused Edie to unpack his words.

He made it to the side of the stage, stood next to De'Vyne and asked what he'd missed? The Mayor's office had awarded Leticia and her team a certificate and plaque of appreciation, along with a check for three thousand dollars as an additional token of gratitude for the successful planning of such a stellar event. Dominic watched as a teary-eyed Leticia stepped to the microphone to express her own heartfelt gratitude and to congratulate the city on such an amazing initiative that is very much needed.

"Well, now that y'all have made me cry and ruined my makeup, let's get back to this party!" Leticia commanded with a laugh.

She walked to the steps and took Dominic's outstretched hand, beaming happily as she went. When she reached the bottom step, Dominic leaned in and kissed her sweetly on the cheek, whispering "Congratulations, Baby," in her ear. De'Vyne grabbed the awards and check from her hand, offering to take them down to the office so Leticia could enjoy the party. Dominic was glad for it because he quickly whisked her out onto the dance floor.

Four years of high school, four Homecoming dances and a senior prom, and this was their first official dance together. Dominic intended to take full advantage. He smoothly moved Leticia around the floor, his hand placed firmly and possessively at the small of her back. The feel of their bodies pressed together and moving in sync for the second time tonight, made a familiar heat form between Leticia's thighs. She quickly tried to think of something else to take her mind off it.

"Is it bad I'm shocked you're such a good dancer?" she asked teasingly.
"And offensive!" Dominic replied, squinting his eyes at her.
"I mean, I've literally never seen you dance before, and I'd definitely never thought I'd be the one dancing *with* you."
"Any time, any place, any song. I'm all yours."

Dominic pulled Leticia's knuckles to his lips and kissed them as he looked longingly into her eyes. This was it. This was the moment they'd both secretly wanted for years, and like a *Hallmark* Christmas miracle, here it was. Leticia's eyes dropped to Dominic's lips, making her hungrily lick her own...a move that did not go unnoticed.

"Hmm," Dominic moaned from deep within his chest. "Soooo, do you have to stay for the *whole* party?"

"Nope," Leticia said, lifting her brows and biting her lip as a sneaky smile formed.

Dominic pulled her closer, sweetly kissed her forehead, then smacked her ass...signaling it was definitely time to go.

ShaRhonda is originally from Maywood, IL, and currently resides in Metro Atlanta, GA. She is a self-proclaimed "Unhinged Creative," as well as owner and operator of S.L.S. Publishing, LLC. She has been published multiple times across various indie publications, including three self-published collections of poetry and a host of other projects.

ShaRhonda holds a Master's Degree from National Louis University in Chicago, and currently works a "cushy 9-5" as a means to fund the dream of being a best-selling author some day.

ShaRhonda often co-writes with her furr-ocious, feline companion, Delilah, who mostly naps through all of their writing sessions.

Follow along on her writing journey & check out her merch brand The S-L-S Collection.